CIRCULATING WITH THE LISTED PROBLEMS(S):

Scribbles on first few pages

3-5-13   AF@GRB

DORA'S SNOWY FOREST ADVENTURE

adapted by Lauryn Silverhardt
illustrated by Robert Roper

Ready-to-Read

Simon Spotlight/Nick Jr.
New York   London   Toronto   Sydney

Based on the TV series *Dora the Explorer*® as seen on Nick Jr.®

SIMON SPOTLIGHT
An imprint of Simon & Schuster Children's Publishing Division
1230 Avenue of the Americas, New York, New York 10020
© 2008 Viacom International Inc. All rights reserved. NICK JR., *Dora the Explorer*, and all
related titles, logos, and characters are registered trademarks of Viacom International Inc.
All rights reserved, including the right of reproduction in whole or in part in any form.
SIMON SPOTLIGHT, READY-TO-READ, and colophon are registered trademarks of
Simon & Schuster, Inc.
Manufactured in the United States of America
6 8 10 9 7 5
Library of Congress Cataloging-in-Publication Data
Silverhardt, Lauryn.
Dora's snowy forest adventure / by Lauryn Silverhardt ; illustrated by Robert Roper. — 1st ed.
p. cm. — (Ready-to-read ; #18)
"Based on the TV series Dora the Explorer as seen on Nick Jr."—Copyright p.
ISBN-13: 978-1-4169-5865-9
ISBN-10: 1-4169-5865-7
I. Roper, Robert. II. Dora the explorer (Television program) III. Title.
PZ7.S58585Dor 2008'
[E]—dc22
2007037837

Hi! I am . I am going

to read a story.

Do you like  ?

Me too!

Once upon a time there was a
SNOW PRINCESS

who lived in a Magic 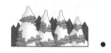 .
SNOWY FOREST

"Look,  ," says .

DORA   BOOTS

"Someone is trying

to get out of your !"

BOOK

"Hi! My name is  .

SNOW FAIRY

I need to find the

SNOW PRINCESS
and save

the Magic

SNOWY FOREST ."

"A  waved
WITCH

her
MAGIC WAND

and locked the
SNOW PRINCESS

in a  .
TOWER

With the  gone,

SNOW PRINCESS

the Magic

SNOWY FOREST

is starting to melt!"

Then  adds,

SNOW FAIRY

"If the

SNOW PRINCESS

smiles into a magic 💎 ,

CRYSTAL

it will start to ❄ again!"

SNOW

BOOTS

and I will help

save the .
SNOW PRINCESS

Who do we ask for help

when we don't know where

to go?

Yeah, !

MAP

 says we need to go

MAP

across the ,

ICY OCEAN

past the ,

SNOWY HILLS

and through the .

DARK CAVE

The
PIRATE PIGGIES

will take us across the
ICY OCEAN

in their .
PIRATE SHIP

Watch out for the !
SEA SNAKE

We made it!

Now we need to find a way

down the .

SNOWY HILLS

"Look! Maybe that girl can help us," says .

BOOTS

"Hi! My name is .
PAJ

I can take you to the 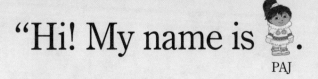!
DARK CAVE

Jump on my !"
DOG SLED

Thanks, .
PAJ

That was great!

Now I see the .
DARK CAVE

Come on!

We made it through

the .

DARK CAVE

Look! I see the !

TOWER

Hooray! We made it
to the .
TOWER

I see the !
WITCH

We need to hurry.

We found the  !
SNOW PRINCESS

But the  cast a spell
WITCH

on her!

She cannot  .
SMILE

Maybe if we all  SMILE

into the magic CRYSTAL,

we can break the spell.

SMILE with us!

One, two, three– SMILE !

Yay! We did it!

The  is free!

SNOW PRINCESS

The Magic SNOWY FOREST

is saved!

Thank you for helping us

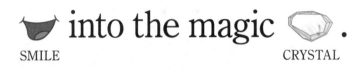 into the magic  .

SMILE   CRYSTAL

We broke the spell!